READING CHAMPION

MORE!

by Enid Richmont and Shahab Shamshirsaz

W
FRANKLIN WATTS
LONDON•SYDNEY

Chapter 1

Sanjay was hungry. His dad and mum were hungry, too. Even their goat was hungry. The rains had not come this year so the ground was dry and the crops had not grown.

One day, Sanjay took the goat up to the hills to look for grass. They searched for hours, but found just a few tufts.

When it was lunchtime, Sanjay sat down to eat.

He pulled a crust of bread out of his pocket.

It was all he had.

Sanjay was just about to eat when an old woman came stumbling towards him.

She was holding a begging bowl in one hand.

She stretched out her other hand to Sanjay.

"I'm hungry," she said.

"Please, spare me some bread."

Sanjay was hungry too, but he was a kind boy

so he broke off some of his crust and held it out.

There was a flash of light and the old woman turned into a golden goddess.

"You have been kind to me," said the goddess. "Now I will repay you. Take this bowl and you will never be hungry again. It will give you whatever food you wish for.

But always remember to thank me."

Then she vanished.

Sanjay looked at the bowl.

It was just like one of his mum's.

Sanjay decided to try out the magic so he wished

for some mangoes. Lo and behold, mangoes

started appearing in the bowl.

"Wow!" gasped Sanjay. He remembered to say,

"Thank you, Goddess" and the bowl stopped.

Chapter 2

Sanjay rushed home to tell his parents.

"It's just a kitchen bowl," said Mum.

"Watch," said Sanjay. "I'll show you."

He wished for curry with rice.

He wished for mangoes and a watermelon.

"Oh!" gasped Mum.

"Thank you, Goddess," said Sanjay,

and the bowl stopped.

Now they had food every day.

Mum's thin cheeks grew round and rosy,

and Dad started to smile again.

They began sharing their good luck

with their hungry neighbours.

And they always remembered

to thank the goddess.

Stories of the magic bowl spread

from village to village.

In the city there lived a Maharajah.

He was greedy and he never said thank you.

One day he heard the news about the magic bowl.

"A magic bowl?" he thought. "This I have to see!"

An elephant carried him to Sanjay's house.

Two servants blew trumpets as he arrived.

"His Highness the Maharajah has come
for supper," they announced.

Sanjay smiled and began to wish.

Soon the table was covered with food –

melon slices, heaps of rice, an enormous bowl

of chicken curry and the most delicious sweets.

"Thank you, Goddess," said Sanjay and the bowl

stopped. "You must always thank the goddess,"

Sanjay explained to the Maharajah.

The Maharajah stroked his fat tummy.

Then he turned to Sanjay. "That bowl is far

too precious to stay here with you," he said.

"Only an important man like *me* can give it

the home it deserves."

Chapter 3

So the Maharajah took the bowl back to
his palace. He couldn't wait to try it out.
He wished for melons and mangoes.
"Yummy!" he said, greedily. "More!"

He wished for samosas and poppadums.

The Maharajah clapped his hands with delight.

"MORE!" he cried. "MORE!"

He wished for curries and rice.

He wished for ice cream and sweets.

"MORE!" he giggled. "MORE!"

Soon the Maharajah had more than enough food

to eat. "Stop!" he ordered the bowl.

But he didn't say thank you to the goddess

so the piles of food kept growing.

Mounds of mangoes and melons rose higher

and higher, and towers of poppadums

and samosas touched the ceiling.

The Maharajah called for his servants.

"Take this food away," he yelled.

But the food poured out of the door

and through the palace.

Chapter 4

The goddess went to visit Sanjay.

"Where is your bowl?" she asked.

"The Maharajah took it," sighed Sanjay.

"Well go and get it back,"

the goddess commanded.

"And take with you

all the poor people that

you can find."

Sanjay gathered the mums, dads and hungry children from the village. He led them in a procession to the Maharajah's palace.

Sanjay looked at all the food.

"Thank you, Goddess," he whispered.

At once, the curries and rice, poppadums and samosas, mangoes and ice cream and sweets stopped filling up the bowl.

The Maharajah's daughter helped set out
the food in the palace gardens. The Maharajah
watched as everyone sat down to eat.

"Thank you, Maharajah," Sanjay called up to him.

"Now please may I have my bowl back?"

The Maharajah's face turned purple with rage.

"Take it!" he roared, and he threw it down,

shattering it into pieces.

Suddenly, it started to rain and out of each fragment of the bowl grew a tiny green shoot. Sanjay smiled. "Thank you, Goddess!" he cried. The people began scooping up the little seedlings. "We can plant these," Sanjay said to them. "We can grow our own crops!"

Sanjay grew lots of crops and became

a rich farmer. He married the Maharajah's daughter,

and he and his family were never hungry again.

Things to think about

1. Why does the goddess give Sanjay the bowl?
2. Can you think of any other stories where food is made by magic?
3. Why do you think the bowl worked so well for Sanjay?
4. Why do you think the Maharajah smashes the bowl at the end of the story?
5. This story has a lesson – what do you think the lesson might be?

Write it yourself

One of the themes of this story is that kindness is rewarded. Can you write a story with a similar theme?

Plan your story before you begin to write it.
Start off with a story map:
• a beginning to introduce the characters and where your story is set (the setting);
• a problem which the main characters will need to fix;
• an ending where the problems are resolved.

Get writing! Try to use interesting noun phrases, such as "the most delicious sweets", to describe your story world and excite your reader.

Notes for parents and carers

Independent reading

This series is designed to provide an opportunity for your child to read independently, for pleasure and enjoyment. These notes are written for you to help your child make the most of this book.

About the book

Sanjay is poor and hungry, He is also very kind. When he agrees to share the last of his food with an old woman, he is rewarded by a goddess with a magic bowl. Then the greedy Maharajah steals the bowl, but he is unable to control the magic ...

Before reading

Ask your child why they have selected this book. Look at the title and blurb together. What do they think it will be about? Do they think they will like it?

During reading

Encourage your child to read independently. If they get stuck on a word, remind them that they can sound it out in syllable chunks. They can also read on in the sentence and think about what would make sense.

After reading

Support comprehension and help your child think about the messages in the book that go beyond the story, using the questions on the page opposite.

Give your child a chance to respond to the story, asking:

Did you enjoy the story and why?

Who was your favourite character?

What was your favourite part?

What did you expect to happen at the end?

Franklin Watts
First published in Great Britain in 2018
by The Watts Publishing Group

Series Editors: Jackie Hamley and Melanie Palmer
Series Advisors: Dr Sue Bodman and Glen Franklin
Series Designer: Peter Scoulding

A CIP catalogue record for this book is
available from the British Library.

ISBN 978 1 4451 6243 0 (hbk)
ISBN 978 1 4451 6279 9 (pbk)
ISBN 978 1 4451 6280 5 (library ebook)

Printed in China

Franklin Watts
An imprint of
Hachette Children's Group
Part of The Watts Publishing Group
Carmelite House
50 Victoria Embankment
London EC4Y 0DZ

An Hachette UK Company
www.hachette.co.uk

www.franklinwatts.co.uk

For David the Star-Man and Anna the Actress – E.R.